A LIFE OF

BOUNDARIES

Moving Toward Intentional Wholeness

BISHOP CHRISTOPHER JOHNSON

THE GREATNESS COACH LLC.

Dedication

This book is dedicated to my wife, Toya. I love you beyond measure, you have helped me to maintain balance in my life. Thank you for allowing me to be who God called me to be.

Table of Contents

Introduction: The Blessing of Boundaries

"Wholeness invokes balance."

- M. J. Ryan

Wholeness. That is what prompts the pushing of my pen in this work. To achieve it, one must eliminate mediocre pursuits and must not settle for empty pursuits but move toward finding a sense of complete fulfillment in every area of life. Personally, I want to successfully manage everything I have to offer my life, the world around me, and my creator. This is the life of boundaries, one where proper management of time, effort, and resources allows us the opportunity to become the epitome of complete perfection. To achieve it is difficult and at times painful. It requires steady effort and comes with a price. Trust me it is doable. I'm glad you have decided to read this book because it will help you ascertain how to maintain finite control in your life and move toward wholeness. One of the joys of this book is that it covers a wide and extensive range of topics and will draw relevance to multiple people. Boundaries are not just for one area of your life, but in order to move toward wholeness it must be applied in every area.

It has become popular practice to utter statements like "a life with no limits" or "take the limits off," and many of us have tried to make this ideology the driving paradigm that we live by. All over the world people love to think that there is no limit to what they can do. Many of us are infatuated with the idea of endless possibilities and potential. I will admit I was one of those people. I believed that I could do any and every thing, and that there was no limit to what I could achieve. However, it was the range of potential that came into question. I know that "I can do all things through Christ" and I still believe that. But, what I can do and what I will do are different things. The perspectives are different. I know that I can do many things and have the potential to achieve my goals because of the abilities God has granted me. I can play basketball, but with my 5'8 frame and very mediocre skill level I wouldn't be maximizing my effectiveness. I can also sing a little, but that doesn't mean that I am ready for the life of a professional singer and pursue a gospel album. In short, just because you can do something doesn't mean that you should. What we should pursue is the area where we are going to have the maximum amount of results and where we can be the most effective.

This is the difference between can and should. Maybe you have extended yourself in areas where you may have the ability participate in, but are you seeing any results? Are you being effective? Do you feel a sense of fulfillment?

In a sense, we become hoarders of our lives. We have hobbies, activities, and even people that we may hold onto in the slim possibility that one day it will fall into place. This describes a life that has no limits. Always accepting new tasks, allowing new people, and welcoming un-necessary demands on your life are all examples of a life without limits. There are many successful people who adopt this mindset of limitless living. The problem with it is they may think that there are no limits to what they can have or achieve, but sooner or later they will become overwhelmed by the fact that they cannot supply the demand for all of these areas. At some point, something will have to give. Most of the time it will be the person who has no limits or boundaries in his or her life.

2 Chronicles 6:18 says, "But will God really live on earth among people? Why, even the highest heavens cannot contain you."[1] God's power is limitless and so is everything about Him. He is unchallenged in his authority. God is infinite which means he is not held to limits or boundaries. The same is not true for us. We are finite beings with limits and we are held to boundaries whether we agree or not. There are just some things that we just cannot and will not

---

[1] (Bible.com, 2008) 2 Chronicles 6:18, NLT

do. The sooner we realize that there are some limits on our lives, the quicker we can begin to narrow down tasks that we should or should not engage in. Understanding that you have limits will help you keep control in your life and guard against unwanted or unneeded stressors or worries. My father, the great late Bishop T.P. Johnson Sr. transitioned to the next life in 2012. I remember the inscription on the inside of his casket read, "May the Works I've Done Speak for me." At that moment, standing there over my father's body it became clear to me that there was some work that I must complete before my time comes to take the celestial trip. But what work? That would be the question. Like me, many who are reading this book struggle with pinpointing exactly what work we are supposed to be doing because for so long we felt that we can do everything. This is the life of limitless living.

Actually there is specific work for you to do. There are particular people for you to impact; there is a distinct mark that you will make on certain people. Jesus was initially sent to seek and save the lost. Moses was to lead the children of Israel out of Egypt. Saul was sent to minister to the Gentiles. David ministered in his generation.

The danger is in thinking that you are to change every person, help every child, or be everyone's friend. The truth is that you cannot trust everyone, save everyone, or change everyone. There has to be some boundaries drawn. We are limited in helping everyone. God can do all of those things, but we, my friend, are limited. A more beneficial effort may be to selectively set in order certain tasks and certain relationships to foster that may result in your effectiveness than to try and live a life without boundaries and wear yourself thin not being effective in any of them. Setting boundaries will require you to be firm and decisive. For some personality traits this may be difficult.

So what is a life of boundaries? It is thinking long and hard about the possibility of welcoming any new friends because in this season of your life you are so busy that you are not being a good friend to the ones that you have now. It is cutting back on unproductive activities that are fun for you but also futile and empty because there is not sense of fulfillment or production in the activity. It is telling people *no* who wish to occupy your time with pointless activities just to pass the time. It is realizing that you can't save everyone or help everyone and if you continue, you will eventually have nothing to help or give with. Living a life of boundaries is knowing that just because you can do it, doesn't mean that you should. It means that sometimes you have to do what you have to do until you can do what you want to do. If you set boundaries for yourself and your life, it frees you from overextending and over exertion. You will not wear yourself down to the point that you have nothing else to offer. Not only that, when you set boundaries you will always have something left over.

Boundaries allow you to have time left from the day, money left from the month, and energy left over to burn. Consequently, if you have not come to the realization that you need or should have boundaries then the complete opposite may be true in your life. If you have nothing left, always burned out, feeling stressed and over used it is because other things and people have control in your life right now only because you have set no boundaries. As you are reading this book, it is your time to start drawing the lines. You have to give people their limits in your life, if not they will think they have full access and push you to see how far you will go.

The Benefits of Boundaries

In the world of sports, almost every event or match deals with some kind of boundaries. Imagine a track and field event if there were no lines on the track. There would be utter chaos, runners would just run all over the place with no idea where to begin or for relays where the exchange zones are. In football, the lines on the field tell yardage, demark the field of play, and tell where the end zone is. If there were no lines, you really couldn't keep score and it would just be a group of people just playing tackle the man with the football. Some of you may remember when basketball didn't have three point lines, but what if there weren't any lines at all? Players could just run out of bounds as they please and the basic rules of the game would be abandoned and ignored.

If our highways and interstates did not have any lines, there wouldn't be any boundaries for drivers and cars would literally run off the road. Transportation would almost be impossible without numerous accidents. Suffice it to say, boundaries are necessary. We need them to maintain order and balance in our lives. Beyond the basic necessity of them are the benefits of boundaries.

Focus

One of the main benefits of boundaries is that it allows for deeper levels of focus. People without boundaries have the propensity to involve themselves in a little bit of everything while being efficient in very little.

Boundaries reveal certain areas of focus for people who seem to have busy lives. One biblical example of how important focus is Peter, who when prompted to do so gained the strength and courage to step out and walk on water as he had seen Jesus do. While walking on the water, his environment became chaotic.

> "28 Then Peter called to him, "Lord, if it's really you, tell me to come to you, walking on the water." 29 "Yes, come," Jesus said. So Peter went over the side of the boat and walked on the water toward Jesus. 30 But when he saw the strong wind and the waves, he was terrified and began to sink. "Save me, Lord!" he shouted."[2]

Notice in this narrative the power of focus. How does the boundary with focus equate to maximum effectiveness? First, there is a boundary. Peter made a simple notion to Jesus that if it was He that maybe He could have him to come to him on the water. Here in lies the boundary, "Go to Jesus." As he stepped out onto the water Peter was able to

---

[2] (Bible.com, 2008) Matthew 14: 28-30 NLT

do the impossible and walk on the water as he had seen the master do. Here, he was able to perform at maximum potential because his boundary was set and his focus clear- just go to Jesus. Peter's gaze was fixed and his heart was ready. All he had to do was just focus on Jesus and everything else would just fall under his feet. Yet, like so many of us, Peter widened his gaze and opened his boundary. What happened? Peter lost his focus. As he saw the winding of the winds and the warring of the waves, the boundary fell and his focus waivered.

Because many of us have no boundaries in our lives it causes us to fixate our focus on things don't matter. When Peter lost his boundary, he lost his focus, and when he lost his focus, he began to sink. How many of us have had our focus destroyed because we too erased the boundaries in our lives? For example, what about the single mother who finally reached a place where she and the children were happy and making progress, and then someone came along that looked like a husband (but really wasn't fit to be a boyfriend), and she erased a boundary that secured her focus. Or what about the man who was working on getting himself right by going back to school in order to get a better paying job, but the fast money of the street life called his name and the boundary that had him focused on school is now gone and he's back to square one. Boundaries keep us grounded and rooted in the primary objectives of life. Boundary plus focus equals effectiveness.

Eliminate Stressors

There can be a plethora of factors that lead to stress. Factors may range from traumatic events, people, unfavorable conditions, or a constant fear or anxiety. Whatever the case, stressors can come in our lives because we have no boundaries. Some of us have stress that we welcome because we simply just don't draw the line. Sometimes we allow people to dump their problems and pains on us, which in turn result in added stress for our lives. Many of us are occupied doing things that are not adding value, but in actuality are taking away from our goals, dreams, and intentions. Boundaries simply send a clear message about what we need and who we are. Boundaries simply communicate to everyone "this is what I will allow and this is what I will not allow." If you don't set boundaries, people will push themselves without invitation into areas of your life that you have not welcomed. The boundaries will surely benefit you, but they are made for others.

Consider a married couple that creates a boundary in their relationship so no one else could get in the middle of the relationship. Yet, a series of events led to distrust and one of the two removes the boundary. Now an outside party, such as a family member, is in the marriage and holding a grudge against the other party while the couple has decided to move past it. Now this is an added stressor. Before the boundary was removed, no one could penetrate the couple's relationship. Now the outside party is still mad which puts stress on the relationship because the couple is fighting to move on, but the outside party is still dwelling on what happened. A vacant boundary can lead to a broken and troubled relationship.

Now take a father who is very active in his community and has a great deal of respect from the young men in his community, but he also has sons at home. Three other young boys who have no father often share with him their concerns and struggles with having no father present. He feels the obligation to try and help and begins to try and father these three young men, while his sons are home harboring an animosity for their father because he has no boundaries and he wants to help everyone while his own family desires the same attention.

Boundaries help us draw the line and determine to the outside world *this is all I have to offer and this is all I'm willing to give* because anything else would be added stress. When we create and set in place boundaries, it allows us to dictate what to share and does not give others the freedom to take. That's stress that we really don't have to accept.

Maintain Control

There is nothing more disheartening than living your life feeling like you have no control over your thoughts, actions, or condition. When you have no boundaries in your life, it is easy to allow others to control how you feel and how you act. People who have lost control in their lives are those who have surrendered to the moods, methods, and mindsets of others. I must admit that I have been guilty of this throughout my life and it is one of the worst feelings. I have been pastoring now for 10 years and I can remember when I first began in ministry, I would often allow what people said or did shift my whole attitude.

I remember, when as a young pastor, certain people who could walk in the room and automatically change my disposition. This was because inexperience and youth had me in a place with no boundaries. The reason people could spin my emotions is because I allowed it. If someone is having a great day and that attitude is positive, if someone else comes along and tries to change it, the first person has a choice to make. Does he or she stand on that boundary and ignore the person or surrender to the attack on the boundary?

I've learned over the years to only give people access to the part of me that I'm willing to be flexible with. Other areas in my life are non-negotiable. One of the boundaries I had to set was that if I'm someone's pastor, I have to monitor how close I allow that person to get to me. What I have discovered is that everyone can't handle Chris so I have to a give to them their *pastor*. This is not always easy because some people are just so fun to be around, but years of hurt and betrayal have taught me that certain parts of my life are just off limits to everyone. Even Jesus had boundaries of this sort. When he did his most intimate and influential works he would only allow Peter, James, and John to assist him. That is boundary at its best.

If you let them, people will take advantage of your kindness, use your time, and drown you with their miseries. The quicker you realize that you will not be able to help others if you keep allowing too many people have limitless access to you, the more control you will have in your life. I beg you, dear reader, to make the boundary clear. Limit your tears over everyone else's problems. Be an ear but not a sponge. Hear their problems but please don't hold onto them. Learn to let go of the people that God is sending away. Please don't be so naïve as to think that you can provide a shoulder for everyone to cry one because you only have two. Take control back! Let everyone know, these are my limits and this is as far as I will go. Enough is enough!

Step Toward Wholeness

Over my short yet busy years of pastoring, I have noticed that some people get healed but they are still not whole. They will make significant changes in one or two areas in their lives, while other areas are still lacking. I believe that our goal should not only be to live progressive lives, but to seek holistic and complete lives. In his book, *Emotionally Healthy Spirituality*, Peter Scazzero stated:

> "God made us as whole people, in his image (Genesis 1: 27). That image includes physical, spiritual, emotional, intellectual, and social dimensions… Ignoring any aspect of who we are as men and women made in God's image always results in destructive consequences— in our relationship with God, with others, and with ourselves. If you meet someone, for example, who is mentally challenged or physically disabled, his or her lack of mental or physical development is readily apparent. An autistic child in a crowded playground standing alone for hours without interacting with other children stands out. Emotional underdevelopment, however, is not so obvious when we first meet people. Over time, as we become involved with them, that reality becomes readily apparent."[3]

---

[3] (Spirituality, 2006)

From Scazzero's perspective, we must learn how to draw emotional, social, physical, intellectual and spiritual boundaries to prevent an unhealthy state of being. A life without boundaries will give us unrest in each of these areas. Many of us have strict boundaries in one or two of these areas but then lack boundaries in others. These compartments of our being are God given and they must be protected. Many people who have busy lives or have very pressing positions and status will fall prey to this kind of dissented display of emotionalism. If one is not careful, years can pass and the emotional scars will not be recognizable. Many leaders focus on *looking the part,* but deep down they have allowed their emotional and spiritual self to be altered by outside forces. These must be guarded.

In order for wholeness to be achieved, boundaries must be present for each of these divisions. One must have proper boundaries for the mind and spirit with equal provisions. Proper boundaries in your life means spreading limits out evenly in every area of your life. For example, many leaders have no problem being authoritative and stern when it comes to doing their jobs, but then they lose their identity and allow anything to happen in their homes. Many passionate and progressive professionals will do whatever it takes to better themselves to advance up the corporate ladder; however, that same passion is not present when dealing with their marriage. These are the dangers of not moving toward wholeness.

We should desire to have wholeness everyday. Wholeness means that I'm being proficient in marriage, money, and mental capacities. I'm reminded of an instance in the bible where Jesus healed 10 leprous men and he said to one that their faith has "made you whole."[4] Wholeness comes with balance. Balance comes with boundaries. Beloved, my prayer is that all who read this work would understand that boundaries must be set because the quality of your life depends on it. We should not only seek healing but we should most importantly seek wholeness so that we

---

[4] (Bible.com, 2008) Luke 17:19

can be complete people. Our churches, schools, and jobs are filled with people who are simply not whole. There are areas that have been healed and even areas that are healthy, but if there are more areas still broken you will pull from strong areas to supply energy and effort for weak ones. This is not wholeness. Let the boundaries be the blessings for your break through. Like a light flickering in the basement of your soul, your inner fulfillment is trying to find a more dominant force to ignite it.

Let's Take the Journey

Wherever you are in life, whether you are in the working class or a business owner, operating in a crack house or courthouse - I believe that we are all are in search for something. Although our desires may be different, we all desire happiness or some sense of fulfillment. If you are like me, you have many people pulling at you, many people count on you, and you have many hats to wear. You know that your life can get hectic. Many people are autodidacts, or self-taught, and learn to pursue personal growth. Hopefully you will learn that you need boundaries to keep you grounded. It will require some discipline and determination, but I believe that if you take this journey with me you will find very practical ways to implement boundaries in every area of your life that will revolutionize how you live. You are closer to wholeness than you think, buckle down and stay the course, start here and make this boundary number one until you complete this book. Let's begin!

Chapter 1:
Physical Boundaries

"Though it has been variously commended and practiced for centuries, simplicity has seldom been more needed than it is today. Health requires it. Sanity demands it. Contentment facilitates it." [5]

-Richard Swenson

      The busier our lives become, the greater the demand will be on our bodies. More money means more responsibilities. More responsibilities usually result in stress. The reality is that the higher you climb up the

---

[5] (Richard A. Swenson, 2004)

"success" ladder, the greater the demand will be for your time and attention. This may result in very little personal recreation time, or if you have a family that would be family time. This seems to be the great pattern of life. Get busy! Lose sleep! Neglect my body! Repeat! This will lead to a very complicated life, one in which could drain anyone of physical strength and endurance.

Many people have very complicated lives. These are lives that involve spouses, children, multiple jobs, and other commitments. Our commitment to these various areas can complicate things very quickly. This is why we need boundaries because they help to simplify things a little. Multiple demands can make your life chaotic and leave you with sense of overload. Central to setting physical boundaries would be the discipline of taking care of your body. When we allow commitments to take over, often times, what suffers is our bodies. Our bodies, when healthy, benefit from internal peace and relaxation, but when depraved can suffer from depression and discouragement.

Our bodies house all the necessary means to our success. Without it we wouldn't have any physical contact with the world. The bible teaches that man is made up of three parts. Man is body, soul, and spirit. 1 Thessalonians 5:23 says, "Now may the God of peace make you holy in every way, and may your whole spirit and soul and body be kept blameless until our Lord Jesus Christ comes again."[6] Just as it is important for us to have healthy spiritual lives and healthy mental lives, we must take seriously the necessity of personal fitness. No matter how sharp the mind is or how exceptional the intellect, if the body is not properly maintained you will not have energy to operate in excellence on a consistent basis. Best selling author and physician Richard Swenson also mentions having margins in physical energy in his book *Margin*

> WHEN WE DIP into the tank for some physical energy, we all want the ladle to return with something in it. Unfortunately, for too many of us the tank dried up years ago. A large percentage of

---

[6] (Bible.com, 2008)

Americans are sadly out of shape and have diminished physical energy reserves because of poor conditioning. Others, such as mothers of newborns and those who work two jobs, are chronically sleep-deprived. Still others suffer from chronic biscuit poisoning. These three factors—poor conditioning, sleep deprivation, and obesity—constitute a physical energy desert where no margin can grow. Lacking margin in physical energy, we feel under-rested and overwhelmed. With no strength left for our own needs, let alone the needs of others, we put our tiredness to bed hoping tomorrow will be a stronger day. [7]

The risk of a *dry tank* is too big to take. Many of us are guilty of *giving* but have fallen short of taking. The danger in constantly giving is that eventually you will have nothing left to give. Your tank becomes empty. Eventually, you will have to take time out and *take* a break. A great

---

[7] (Richard A. Swenson, 2004)

way to prevent this is to reserve a time that is just for your body maintenance.

It's Your Body

My life moves at a considerably fast pace. My days have to be planned and structured out or else my life would be chaotic. Some people can get away with planning weeks at a time and they are just focused on the objectives for the week. I'm a bit different. I can't wait 5 days before I seek to accomplish a task. This gives me a sense of anxiety because it will come down to the fifth day and I won't have gotten anything done. Instead, I have taken up time doing things for others because I didn't have boundaries for them to respect. I have to get it done right then.

I developed this kind of boundary in my life because I had to learn the hard way that when your body has had enough, it will shut down. Constant headaches, blurred vision, constant bouts of extreme sleepiness, drained energy, weight gain and miniature spurts of depression all came into my life as a direct result of me neglecting my body. I allowed the business of life to stretch me in so many directions that I neglected my physical activity. I believe that there should time reserved on your daily agenda for your physical exercise and eating. If we are going to have any longevity at all, then we must take care of our bodies. It took me a while to realize that no one was particularly interested in how I looked or felt because they just wanted from me what they wanted. I'm the only one concerned about my body. Our bodies are like our vehicles. We can be guilty of just driving and driving while ignoring small signs that there could be something seriously wrong under the hood.

You Can't Do it All

We cannot truly know our limitations or depth of skill set until we have first searched the knowledge of God. I believe that true knowledge of one's self comes from first establishing a healthy and dynamic relationship with God.

There are some things about humanity that only divinity can teach. It was the Apostle Paul who said, "For you died to this life, and your real life is hidden with Christ in God."[8] (Colossians 3:1). I think that this is a crucial step in understanding your limitations. Too many of us look within ourselves to find ourselves and this kind of ideology could lead us to believe that we need no dependency on God. This kind of thought could result to arrogance, pride, and a false sense of self. To gain a clear perspective and a more accurate assessment of our limitations we must always view ourselves in relation to God.

> Augustine wrote in Confessions, in A.D. 400, "How can you draw close to God when you are far from your own self?" He prayed: "Grant, Lord, that I may know myself that I may know thee." Meister Eckhart, a Dominican writer from the thirteenth century, wrote, "No one can know God who does

[8] (Bible.com, 2008)

not first know himself." 1 St. Teresa of Avila wrote in The Way of Perfection: "Almost all problems in the spiritual life stem from a lack of self-knowledge." John Calvin in 1530 wrote in his opening of his Institutes of the Christian Religion: "Our wisdom . . . consists almost entirely of two parts: the knowledge of God and of ourselves. But as these are connected together by many ties, it is not easy to determine which of the two precedes and gives birth to the other." [9]

Only then can we begin to realize that we can't do it all. It is better to be free from everyone's expectations by setting clear boundaries for everyone. If you don't set them, people will misuse, mishandle, and mistake you. My daily dependency on God reminds me that I'm limited. This helps me to communicate that same thing to others. I have limited time, resources, plans, energy, and skills. I don't have the capacity to be everything for everyone. I can only give but so much, work but so much, provide but so much,

---

[9] (Spirituality, 2006)

I don't have an endless supply of anything! These are all boundaries that need to be set in order to maintain or even shoot for a place of wholeness. Don't put extra or unnecessary physical demands on your body because after all, it's yours and it's the only one you have. You don't have to jump at the last minute just because someone calls, knowing that you have had limited time for yourself. You can't be everyone's parents in the neighborhood while you still have children you are raising. You can't pay bills in multiple households, nor counsel everyone else's relationships while you lay alone and unhappy. You don't have to jump at your families' beckoning call when you have some things personally that you are working on. Set some boundaries, don't literally run your physical health and body in the ground because you failed to say *that's enough, I can't do everything!*

Okay, so let's try and assess where you are. Grab a sheet of paper and answer the following questions about yourself:

1. Do I feel like I can provide a solution to everyone's problems when they present them to me?
2. Do I feel obligated to help members of my extended family just because they are family?
3. Do I automatically insert myself into the issues of others around me?
4. Do I automatically try and offer solutions without totally knowing the problems?
5. Do I leave projects incomplete or fail to meet time restrictions?
6. Do I normally commit myself to things that I really don't have time to participate in?
7. Am I easily persuaded?

8. Do I find my life going in several different directions?

9. Do I receive a high volume of calls, emails, and text from people needing my assistance?

10. Do I find myself giving out more than I'm taking in?

Rest and Recover

Rest doesn't always mean sleep. Of course sleep is a huge part of resting but some of us who spend a great deal of time using our minds with activities such as planning, administrating, developing, motivating, and mentoring will need time to just recover. This could mean just doing absolutely nothing or engaging in activity that requires us not to think. If all my time is spent working or grinding it out, then I will have no time to rest my mind or body. That extra time or space to just do nothing is what

Richard Swenson refers to as *Margin*. For Swenson, living life with margin speaks to the quality of life. Quality of life is determined by how much time or resources we have left over after all of the other demands have been met. If we are so busy that we have no extra time, extra energy, or extra room for recreational thinking or devotion, then we are living a life without boundaries or margin. In his book entitled *Margin* Swenson describes a life without margin as marginless living:

> Marginless is not having time to finish the book you're reading on stress; margin is having the time to read it twice. Marginless is fatigue; margin is energy. Marginless is red ink; margin is black ink. Marginless is hurry; margin is calm. Marginless is anxiety; margin is security. Marginless is culture; margin is counterculture. Marginless is the disease of the new millennium; margin is its cure.[10]

You can only achieve margin when boundaries are set. You must set aside time for rest and recovery. Time must be

---

[10] (Richard A. Swenson, 2004)

reserved to just do absolutely nothing. For me, my personal quiet times are reserved for God. This is my time to worship or maybe meditate on a certain passage-not on content but just pureness of the passage. If your mind is constantly moving, you need this time for stillness. It is what Scazzero calls centering:

> We stop our activity and pause to be with the Living God. Scripture commands us: "Be still before the LORD and wait patiently for him" (Psalm 37: 7), and "Be still, and know that I am God" (Psalm 46: 10). We move into God's presence and rest there; that alone is no small feat. There are times when I pause for my midday prayer and find that I spend the entire time available— be it five or twenty minutes— centering so I can let go of my tensions, distractions, and sensations and begin resting in the love of God. [11]

---

[11] (Spirituality, 2006)

My wife and I will also have what we call "lazy days." These are days that we do nothing but lay around the house, watch movies, turn off the phones, and do very little thinking or planning. This helps us to refuel and mentally just unwind. As I mentioned earlier, rest doesn't always mean that you are sleeping but for people with very physically demanding responsibilities, sleep is a must. The purpose here is not to give you statistical research and scientific evidence on how much sleep you should be getting, but give you sound advice from my own experiences about depriving yourself of proper rest.

Don't get caught in a web of shame spun by other people. A good night's sleep is not an embarrassment. It's not necessary to feel guilty if you are well rested. Sleep was God's idea. He created the necessity, and "he grants sleep to those he loves." The need for sleep is undeniable and should be regarded as an ally, not an enemy. To sleep soundly for a full night is a valuable restorative gift. As anyone who has read Proverbs knows, however, the sluggard is left defenseless by Scripture.[12]

Maybe you are saying right now, "I don't have that kind of time to rest or to sleep a lot." I want to send this warning out to you; eventually you are going to burn out and your body will shut down on you. It may be fitting for you to consult with your physician to determine the amount of sleep and rest you need based on your workload. Afterward, the responsibility will be on you to draw necessary boundaries and make time for rest and recovery. Put it as one of the top priorities for your day and don't allow anyone or anything to interfere with it. Take quarterly vacations or weekend rest periods. These will keep you fresh and assertive.

In conclusion, the boundary of physicality is crucial. In order to achieve this and to do so effectively, you will have to be adamant about your health. I urge you

---

[12] (Richard A. Swenson, 2004)

to take control of your life and hold yourself accountable. If you are in a leadership position that has you in the public eye, remember that you have a responsibility to look presentable. Hold a standard for yourself in that regard. If the nature of your job, ministry, or role is to provide hope, help, or inspiration to people, then you have to be healthy and sharp to be able do that at a greater level. I want to be clear on the fact that this chapter is not about you being lazy. It is not about you spending your time sleeping and laying around all the time. I'm simply aiming at the idea of balance. We all are trying to find it. We all are trying to find out how much to give here how much to take there. I'm fully aware that in many cases we would love to balance everything and get the proper rest, sleep, and relaxation that is needed. However, some of us have situations that restrict our time and in most cases move us from the proximity of balance. I agree with Chip Heath in *Switch* when he said "What looks like a people problem is often a situation problem" (Heath 2012).[13] Many of you

---

[13] (Heath, 2012)

will argue that your situation has placed a demand on your life that requires your time, talents, and treasures. It may be hard for you to change this dynamic of rest and recovery but it will require you setting some firm boundaries for your health.

Chapter 2:
Emotional Boundaries

"Emotions do not authenticate truth, but emotions do authenticate our understanding and integration of truth"[14]

- David Eckman

By nature we are emotional beings. Our actions and behavior are often fueled by our emotions, which displays our true feelings toward our circumstances or our state of being in those circumstances. Some men are taught from childhood that we should refrain from showing emotion or to be specific, we were to refrain from showing certain emotions. For example, most men were told that men aren't

---

[14] (Eckman, 1995 (Eckman, 2005))

supposed to cry because it is a sign of weakness. The truth
is that we are all emotional. The emotions of sadness,
happiness, giddiness, anger, love, passion, and fear are all
examples of emotions that make up the best part of us.
Imagine being in this world without an emotive of being. If
we didn't have any emotions, we would all walk around
like robots. If we could not feel or show emotions, it would
be a cold dry place without much to get excited about.
Being emotional is nothing to apologize about. God is
emotional. He loves, He is compassionate, He gets angry,
He is grieved, and He is jealous. Since we are made in His
likeness and in His image then we too will be replete with
the same things.

We know that we are going to be emotional whether
good or bad, holy or unholy, saved or un-saved; however,
many of our problems arise when our emotions control us.
When we allow our emotions to get the best of us, then we
are just going along for the ride on this emotional roller

coaster. Some days we are happy, other days, sad. Some days we do not have a care in the world, then others we are anxious for everything. An emotionally unhealthy or unstable person misses out on the chance of being whole. Perhaps what desperately needs to be renovated, is our emotional selves. You may be reading this book and experiencing an emotional unrest right now. It may be that you have no boundaries for your emotions. Emotional boundaries will give you a peace of mind about some things and it will restore the best part of you, which is your ability to feel and connect emotionally. I will admit that the tough part is you knowing that you are the one that needs emotional boundaries in your life. The first step to problem solving is to first realize that you have one. It was Peter Scezzaro in his book *Emotionally Healthy Spirituality* who outlines ten symptoms of an emotionally unhealthy person:

1. Using God to run from God
2. Ignoring the emotions of anger, sadness, and fear
3. Dying to the wrong things
4. Denying the past's impact on the present

5. Dividing our lives into 'secular' and 'sacred' compartments

6. Doing for God instead of being with God

7. Spiritualizing away conflict

8. Covering over brokenness, weakness, and failure

9. Living without limits

10. Judging other people's spiritual journey[15]

Many emotionally unhealthy people stay busy with God's work to appease themselves or others instead of pleasing God. They also will often ignore or cover up the fact that they have issues with sadness and fear. This gives them a false sense of their condition. They will always die to the wrong things. They will often feel as though they have to die to the public weakness instead of the private sins that emotionally bring destruction. If you have ever met a person that has no emotional boundaries, they will deny the

---

[15] (Spirituality, 2006)

impact that the past has on their present. Something has happened to this person that is influencing what is currently taking place, but because they are emotionally unstable they will often try to deny the fact that the past is still very much affecting the present. They will habitually live divided lives with a good side and a bad side.

There are also many individuals who hold leadership positions in churches who operate in several roles and enjoy the perks of doing for God rather than just being with God.

One of the most common symptoms of an individual without emotional boundaries is that person's propensity to spiritualize away conflict or flaws. I admit that there are some times that we must stop, drop, and pray. Then there are other times that we must stand up in the authority of God and confront some issues. In order to avoid conflict emotionally debilitated people will begin to put spiritual connotations and connections on every conflicting idea. This kind of person has allowed people to rape them emotionally and highjack their peace and their emotions have been distributed across a plain of people for their controlling and convenience. As a result, they will often try and cover up their weaknesses and feel a need to prove who they are and will often try to over talk people and they have very minimal listening skills. Out of guilt and shame, they would not have people to see the real emotional wreck they are. So they try to cover it up by trying to appear better than what they are. They ramble on about their accomplishments, they always share their strong moments in life but aren't really willing to tackle the weaker areas. They have to appear strong when actually they are emotionally weak. Other than sharing their weaknesses, they will be open books. People with delicate emotions will live life without limits. No boundaries. They will stretch themselves beyond measure. They will give with no take. This leads to a cycle of emptiness. When they are empty, they are used to seeing other people wear the joy they loaned them, or the love that was stolen from them. This opens them up to a very critical and judgmental way of thinking. If you are to avoid being that kind of person, then you must have emotional boundaries.

Processing Problems: 3 Questions to Ask

"Nobody knows the trouble I've seen, nobody knows my sorrow," these are the words of an old Negro spiritual but I believe they describe the sentiment of so many of us today. Our problems often leave us in emotional turmoil, which leads to other issues such as stress, depression, or anxiety. In most cases, it is not the definition or description of what a problem is that becomes our issue. It is the processing of problems and potential problems that keeps us in an emotional conundrum. There are three questions that you can ask yourself when attempting to process problems that you currently have or will potentially have.

How Long?

The first question is "How Long?" How long will I stay emotionally involved in this problem? How long have I been dealing with this? The answer to this question is actually a boundary that you can implement to this emotional trap. Have you spent the last three days, months, or years on this problem? The longer you allow problems to be present in your mind or in your life, the more vulnerable you are and the more attractive you are to emotional leaches. A certain mount of crying, grieving, and observance is necessary. These things help you to cope and it is part of the healing process. Ecclesiastes 3:1-8 says,

> "1 For everything there is a season,
>
> a time for every activity under heaven.
>
> 2 A time to be born and a time to die.
>
> a time to plant and a time to harvest.
>
> 3 A time to kill and a time to heal.
>
> a time to tear down and a time to build up.
>
> 4 A time to cry and a time to laugh.
>
> a time to grieve and a time to dance.
>
> 5 A time to scatter stones and a time to
gather stones.
>
> a time to embrace and a time to turn away.

6 A time to search and a time to quit searching.

a time to keep and a time to throw away.

7 A time to tear and a time to mend.

A time to be quiet and a time to speak.

8 A time to love and a time to hate.

a time for war and a time for peace."[16]

There is a time for everything. Are you crying when you should be laughing? Are you angry when you should be happy? Are you keeping what you should be throwing away? If yes, how long will you stay in this kind of dilemma? So the question is quite simple, how long will it take? How long are you going to give this current problem? How long will you cry over it? How long will it have control of your life?

---

[16] (Bible.com, 2008)

Can I Fix It?

Problems will linger if you don't deal with them mentally and emotionally. Processing problems doesn't have to be a long drawn out activity. Some problems are easier to process than others. So after you have determined how long you are going to give attention to the problem, you must move to the next question. Can I fix it? I believe that many problems would be temporary if we could check each problem at the door of our lives. These problems can happen suddenly, or they can be a gradual issue that you were invited emotionally to take part in. The sudden sickness of a loved one, bad news on the job, and a betrayal in a relationship are all problems that need to be confronted with the question "Can I fix it?" The answer to this question could determine how long you should dwell in this season of life. What has been healthy practice for me is to ask this question and then conclude that if I can't fix it, then there is no need for me to give attention to this problem any longer. If there is a problem that is beyond my human capacity to fix, then I have to give minimal attention to the problem and lay trust in someone who is higher and stronger than I am. You see, worrying and carrying the load of an issue that you can't fix is a recipe for emotional breakdown. I had to resolve that if I cannot not make it better or fix the situation, then I have to rely on a greater power. For me, that greater power is God. I've learned to strain my emotions on something that I have a little more control in. My father was stricken with cancer in 2012 and there was nothing I could do about it. I did feel sadness and hurt for him, but I could not shoulder nor take on the load because I didn't cause it and I could not change it. At most, I could only pray and keep hoping and stay positive for him. That was a boundary that I had to draw for myself. That was in God's hands. My advice to you would be to release your problems that you cannot fix to the Lord. "Give all your worries and cares to God, for he cares about you." (1 Peter 5:7)[17]

---

[17] (Bible.com, 2008)

Am I the Problem?

As I mentioned earlier, when someone is emotionally unhealthy they will attempt to cover up their flaws and weakness out of embarrassment and shame. Many of us are so emotionally unstable that we are unaware that we can be our biggest problem. How many of us are emotionally healthy enough to say without restraint, I'm the problem. Lets notice this passage from the book of Jonah:

> 3 But Jonah got up and went in the opposite direction to get away from the lord. He went down to the port of Joppa, where he found a ship leaving for Tarshish. He bought a ticket and went on board, hoping to escape from the lord by sailing to Tarshish. 4 But the lord hurled a powerful wind over the sea, causing a violent storm that threatened to break the ship apart. 5 Fearing for their lives, the

desperate sailors shouted to their gods for help and threw the cargo overboard to lighten the ship. But all this time Jonah was sound asleep down in the hold. 6 So the captain went down after him. "How can you sleep at a time like this?" he shouted. "Get up and pray to your god! Maybe he will pay attention to us and spare our lives." 7 Then the crew cast lots to see which of them had offended the gods and caused the terrible storm. When they did this, the lots identified Jonah as the culprit. 8 "Why has this awful storm come down on us?" they demanded. "Who are you? What is your line of work? What country are you from? What is your nationality?"9 Jonah answered, "I am a Hebrew, and I worship the lord, the God of heaven, who made the sea and the land."10 The sailors were terrified when they heard this, for he had already told them he was running away from the lord. "Oh, why did you do it?" they groaned. 11 And since the storm was getting worse all the time, they asked him, "What should we do to you to stop this storm?"

12 "Throw me into the sea," Jonah said, "and it will become calm again. I know that this terrible storm is all my fault." (Jonah 1:3-12)[18]

In this passage Jonah was an emotional mess. God told him to go one way but he ends up going the wrong way. He was fearful of the people he was going to preach to. He was nervous enough to flee from the place God told him to go but then calm enough to go to sleep in a ship with very boisterous winds. It is this rise and fall of emotions that seems identical to many of us at times. As he slept, the other passengers on the ship wanted to know how he could sleep during the storm. These men had sailed these waters before and apparently did not have any troubles before but then Jonah gets on their ship and they encounter a storm. Curious as to why they were catching so much friction, the

---

[18] (Bible.com, 2008)

men wanted more information on Jonah. Jonah could have blamed it on God for sending him to a city called Ninevah. He could have blamed the men for such a small boat. Instead, Jonah said, "It's me." Throw me over board. Part of processing the problem is to always make sure that you are not part of or the problem. To be emotional secure, we have to be willing and ready to admit when we are the ones with the problem. Everything is not everyone else's fault. When you find yourself faced with a problem, can you ask yourself the question, "Am I the Problem?"

Moving Toward Emotional Maturity

It should be our common practice and pursuit to mature emotionally and spiritually. In Ephesians 4:13 it says, "This will continue until we all come to such unity in our faith and knowledge of God's Son that we will be mature in the Lord, measuring up to the full and complete standard of Christ."[19] If our lives are to be whole, our emotions must become mature. Many people are

---

[19] (Bible.com, 2008)

chronologically older, but they are emotionally immature. Scezzaro distinguishes between emotionally immature and mature individuals:

EMOTIONAL INFANTS
- Look for others to take care of them
- Have great difficulty entering into the world of others
- Are driven by need for instant gratification
- Use others as objects to meet their needs

EMOTIONAL CHILDREN
- Are content and happy as long as they receive what they want
- Unravel quickly from stress, disappointments, trials
- Interpret disagreements as personal offenses

- Are easily hurt
- Complain, withdraw, manipulate, take revenge, become sarcastic when they don't get their way
- Have great difficulty calmly discussing their needs and wants in a mature, loving way

EMOTIONAL ADOLESCENTS

- Tend to often be defensive
- Are threatened and alarmed by criticism
- Keep score of what they give so they can ask for something later in return
- Deal with conflict poorly, often blaming, appeasing, going to a third party, pouting, or ignoring the issue entirely
- Become preoccupied with themselves

- Have great difficulty truly listening to another person's pain, disappointments, or needs
- Are critical and judgmental

EMOTIONAL ADULTS

- Are able to ask for what they need, want, or prefer— clearly, directly, honestly
- Recognize, manage, and take responsibility for their own thoughts and feelings
- Can, when under stress, state their own beliefs and values without becoming adversarial
- Respect others without having to change them

- Give people room to make mistakes and not be perfect
- Appreciate people for who they are— the good, bad, and ugly— not for what they give back
- Accurately assess their own limits, strengths, and weaknesses and are able to freely discuss them with others
- Are deeply in tune with their own emotional world and able to enter into the feelings, needs, and concerns of others without losing themselves
- Have the capacity to resolve conflict [20]

Moving toward wholeness means that we accept the challenge of being emotionally responsible adults. If we don't draw emotional boundaries then our emotions will be all over the place. It's not enough to be an adamant church-

---

[20] (Spirituality, 2006)

goer, or to be able to quote ten different scriptures, or to be on a certain ministry for a long time. To achieve intentional wholeness we have to set real, clear, and consistent emotional boundaries in our lives. Emotionally we should be able to communicate to those around us and say exactly what we need and want. We should be able to help people without getting totally engulfed in the project. We should be able to be honest with ourselves and admit when we have some issues. We should be able to disagree without dis-function and be different without discord. Emotionally we should be able to respect others' thoughts and opinions without having to change them. An emotionally healthy person is a person who is emotionally mature and this is the key to becoming a whole person.

Changing Your Mind

In all of my years of teaching, preaching, and pastoring I must admit the hardest thing to do is to get people to change their thinking. Normally if a person changes their mindset then what follows is a change in behavior. Preaching is a spiritual practice that is done under the auspices of the Holy Spirit but it is still highly psychological. The apostle Paul reminds us in Romans 12:2 that we should be "transformed by the renewing of our minds." This bespeaks the idea that if true change is to take place that it must happen in our minds first. I know that placing emotional boundaries in your life is a tough concept to embrace at first but it simply requires you to change your mind in some areas of your life. You are not just changing your mind to be inconsistent and unbalanced but you are changing your mind because it is going to make room for you to grow. In her book *The New Psychology of Success* Carol Dweck notes two contrasting ideas regarding mindsets:

> "Believing that your qualities are carved in stone- the fixed mindset- creates an urgency to prove yourself over and over… The growth mindset is based on the belief that your basic qualities are things you can cultivate through your efforts.

> Although people may differ in every which way- in
> their initial talents and aptitudes, interests or
> temperaments- everyone can change and grow
> through application and experience."[21]

Note how she drew a distinction between a fixed mindset
and a growth mindset. I encourage you to understand your
limitations but be willing to grow in your purpose. Allow
your mind to grow and expand around the idea that you
have particular plans and purposeful pursuits, and that
everyone will not understand or support the distinct and
definite boundaries that you have placed in and over your
life. If you are emotionally unstable and you have no
boundaries to protect that, simply change your mind!

---

[21] (Carol S. Dweck, 2006)

Chapter 3:
Spiritual Boundaries

"For no Christian can hope to enter the warfare of the ages without learning first to first to rest in Chris and in what He has done, and then, through the strength of the Holy Spirit within, to follow Him in a practical, holy life here on earth."[22]

> -Watchman Knee

In this chapter, we come to the idea of drawing spiritual boundaries. So far, we have not plunged deep into the spiritual waters nor have we used much religious rhetoric. There is a spiritual side to us that if not

---

[22] (Knee, 2009)

strengthened and developed can become weak and immature. Just as there are things that can aide in our spiritual growth, there are also things that can contribute to our spiritual decay. What will stunt your spiritual maturity and maintenance quicker than anything is the lack of spiritual boundaries in your life. When everything else has priority and you forget to grow spiritually, it leaves you in a state of dependency on people for an inner peace that only your spiritual connection with God can give you. Lines have to be drawn so that people, people, things, or pursuits will not get in the way of the first thing and that is spiritual communion with God. We must not underestimate the criticality of our spiritual upkeep because it is how we have connection with our creator. Our identity comes from God for Colossians 3:3 reminds us that, "you died to this life, and your real life is hidden with Christ in God."[23] Not only is our identity found in our time with God, but we also have a blessed assurance in God. Romans 8:16 says, "For his Spirit joins with our spirit to affirm that we are God's

---

[23] (Bible.com, 2008)

children."[24] And we cannot forget that the deepest and purest form of our spirituality is our worship, which is a spiritual communion and adoration to God. Even worship is done in spiritual form. John 4:4 says, "For God is Spirit, so those who worship him must worship in spirit and in truth."[25] God is a Spirit! Our early verse says that we also have a spirit that bears witness with his spirit. The indication is clear, we have to reserve time and effort for our spiritual selves to be more in tune with our spiritual God. This will help us to maintain balance and move toward wholeness. The concept that every area in my life is healthy can describe wholeness. So lets spend a little time in this chapter talking about how we can develop boundaries for our spiritual lives.

---

[24] (Bible.com, 2008)
[25] (Bible.com, 2008)

It Matters!

Up until recently, I used to say and think that it really didn't matter where you went to church as long as you were getting the sermon every week. Then there are those who hold the position that it doesn't really matter if you even go to church because you can still grow spiritually and have a decent spiritual life without going to church. Well, it does matter *where* you go to church and it does matter *if* you go to church.

First, in almost every city there are a great number of churches which allows for plenty of options for people to choose from. The harsh reality is that in today's culture going to church is just like shopping for a pair of shoes. You can literally choose the size, shape, and color of the church you are looking for. So since you can choose, I wanted to help you make a sound and important decision on how you should choose your church home and whether you should stay at the church you currently attend.

This is a topic that requires more extensive discussion but what would suffice for now is for me to show you why it matters where you go and help you make a decision to stay or leave. I also want to appeal to the individual who feels as though it isn't even necessary to go to church. The bible is replete with references to the church or the body of Christ collectively which supports the idea that we are supposed to assemble.

The bottom line is that it does matter where you go to church and it is an expectation of God that you are to attend a church. Also, every believer has a responsibility to seek God for and grow spiritually. Assembling and congregating are all great ways to support and in some instances expedite the growth process. Boundaries have to be in place when choosing, attending, or functioning in a local church. Let's dive a little deeper.

The Word Matters

The boundaries that must be considered when deciding whether to stay at a church, or go to church is in the essence, effectiveness, and exclusivity of the Word of God. Before we go any further, I don't want you to negate the personal responsibility of studying the word of God for yourself. This spiritual discipline must be reserved and considered valuable and necessary for your growth. In his book *Celebration of Christian Disciplines* Richard Foster says:

> Many Christians remain in bondage to fears and anxieties simply because they do not avail themselves in the discipline of study. They may be faithful in church attendance and earnest in fulfilling their religious duties, and still they are not changed. I am not hear speaking only of those who are go through mere religious forms, but of those who are genuinely seeking to worship and obey Jesus Christ as Lord and Master. They may sing with gusto, pray in the Spirit, live as obediently as they know, even receive divine visions and revelations, and yet the tenor of their lives remain unchanged. Why? Because they have never taken

up one the central ways God uses to change us: study.[26]

So in order for us to hold this standard, the principle of study must already be present and active in our lives. You have to know the truth in order to measure falsity. More importantly, in order to grow, proper study of the Word of God must not only be a desire but also a discipline. This should be a boundary that you would gladly live by. The Word of God is first. In it are the mandates for marriage, the lessons for life, and the directives for our destiny. It should be top priority in your life and the top concern when assembling in a corporate setting. Before we even get to worship, and before we concern ourselves with work, we must have a healthy dose of God's Word.

In a corporate setting as it relates to your local assembly, the essence of the Word is crucial. By essence I'm referring to the quality. How is it being presented? Is it

[26] (Foster, 1998)

true? Is it accurate? Most of all-is it good enough for you to receive it? Now I understand that sometimes the messenger and the message can be good but there may be something wrong with the reception of the Word. For the sake of this work, let's consider that recipients are open, ready, and willing to receive but the message lacks substance and quality. There are obvious miscues. Maybe personal issues are hindering the man or woman of God who stands as the vessel. Maybe the messenger has stopped studying or they have stopped seeking to better themselves. Maybe they are chronologically advanced and they may not be the preacher they used to be.

Whatever the case may be, you have to draw some boundaries and make a decision on whether you want to stay there and be spiritually starved or move on and find spiritual nutrients elsewhere. Now this may be especially tough for those who have been in ministries for an extended amount of time and maybe the pastor of the ministry is your relative. The same is true for you, grow or go! Listen to 1 Peter 2:1, "Like newborn babies, you must crave pure spiritual milk so that you will grow into a full experience of salvation. Cry out for this nourishment"[27] Imagine if babies would nurse on bad milk. What if the milk wasn't processed right or if the impurities from the mother's body would taint the milk and therefore be a detriment to the baby? In the above scripture, Peter implies that we (like the baby) should desire the word of God. If the church we attend has a vessel that taints the milk it can harm us. He says we should "cry out" for nourishment. We should have a desire for the word above all else because just as the baby is getting milk to grow, so is the believer that takes in the Word of God. This is why the essence of the Word matters. What happens to it between the Holy Spirit's prompting and the proclamation of it across the pulpit? This should be a boundary you are willing to draw. Your life depends on it. Your spiritual growth depends on it! Feeding your spirit starts here. Jesus is the "bread" of life. He is also the "Word" of God. He is perfect in all of His

---

[27] (Bible.com, 2008)

ways. Sometimes the vessel can misinterpret, misrepresent, and mishandle the Word. You have to draw this boundary because you can be guilty of swelling with redundant knowledge but not growing. Swelling is not growth; it only gives the appearance of growth.

The effectiveness of the Word is important also. It doesn't matter how long you have been going to the ministry or involved in the various groups. What begs asking is, is the Word effective in your life? Are you different because of the word? Are you getting instructions for your life? Are you challenged to live better? Are you uncomfortable sometimes when listening? If you answered no to these, then the Word coming forth is not effective. Again, there is nothing wrong with the spiritual food; it's just the way it's been prepared. The word should be so effective that you would not do anything in your life or at the ministry that would go against God's holy script. You won't be ashamed of the gospel because you understand that it is the "power of God unto salvation." Effective messages will cause you to be more than just hearers of the Word but as James 1:22 says, "But don't just listen to

God's word. You must do what it says. Otherwise, you are only fooling yourselves."[28] When you have a messenger that gives effective sermons then you will leave not only with the information but with inspiration to do something.

Finally, the Word of God should be exclusive. It should be guarded and protected as the central element in your life. Don't get caught up in the glitz and glamour that sometimes comes with church performances and presentations. Don't allow the industry to trump ministry. Stay true to the Word of God. It should be exclusively the only thing in your life that you give absolute and total pliability to. If God said it in his Word then that should just settle it. Don't allow people to sway you to the right or to the left. You should be more mature than that. Don't allow people to persuade you to live unhealthy lifestyles, stand on God's Word. Hide it in your heart, and holster it so that when you need it, it is easily accessible.

---

[28] (Bible.com, 2008)

Stand your ground, putting on the belt of truth and the body armor of God's righteousness. For shoes, put on the peace that comes from the Good News so that you will be fully prepared. 16In addition to all of these, hold up the shield of faith to stop the fiery arrows of the devil. Put on salvation as your helmet, and take the sword of the Spirit, which is the word of God. (Ephesians 6:14-17)[29]

Worship Matters

Boundaries must also be set for and around your personal and public worship. Because of the intimate nature of worship, it is very necessary and central to spiritual health. To even begin to fathom the true nature of spirituality, we must be willing to yield to the demands and requirements of spiritual enlightenment. The reverence and respect given to the divine appropriates our hearts and teaches us to have dependency on someone greater than we

---

[29] (Bible.com, 2008)

are. In his book *Real Worship* Warren Wiersbe gives a working definition of worship:

> Worship is the believers' response of all that they are—mind, emotions, will, and body—to what God is and says and does. This response has its mystical side in subjective experience and its practical side in objective obedience to God's revealed will. Worship is a loving response that's balanced by the fear of the Lord, and it is a deepening response as the believer comes to know God better. And what should be the result of all this? Transformation…"[30]

Worship is a response. It is humanity's response to divinity and all of the special interests that divinity has in humanity. Being that we have a spiritual side, it is important for us to give to our God the adoration and exaltation that he deserves. This ardent worship feeds our spiritual side. This is vitally important to the whole idea of wholeness. Earlier

---

[30] (Wiersbe, 2011)

in this book we mentioned the need for our bodies and emotions to be healthy in order to move toward wholeness. When we add spirituality to that list we complete the make up of man's being. This sense of self-awareness is something that is pretty widely agreed upon in both the religious circles and in the secular educational systems. In the bible, 1 Thessalonians 5: 23 mentions three parts to our being, "Now may the God of peace make you holy in every way, and may your whole spirit and soul and body be kept blameless until our Lord Jesus Christ comes again."[31] The apostle Paul mentions three portions of whole humanity and that is body, soul, and spirit. In a similar fashion, Australian neurologist and father of psychoanalysis Sigmund Freud goes on to describe the id, ego, and super-ego which can be compared to the bible's body (id), ego (soul), and super-ego (spirit). Here we see that even from a spiritual side or from a very practical and scientific perspective that the spirituality of a person is vitally

---

[31] (Bible.com, 2008)

important. In his book *the Ego and the Super-Ego*, Freud
said,

> "If the ego were merely the part of the id that is
> modified by the influence of the perceptual system,
> the representative in the mind of the real external
> world, we should have a simple state of things to
> deal with. But there is a further complication. The
> considerations that led us to assume the existence of
> a differentiating grade within the ego, which may be
> called the ego-ideal or super-ego, have been set
> forth elsewhere. They still hold good. The new
> proposition which must now be gone into is that this
> part of the ego is less closely connected with
> consciousness than the rest. [32]

From the above statements stems the idea that while the
soul and body are connected to the body, they differ in
functionality. Just as I have encouraged you to guard your

---

[32] (Freud)

health and your body, the same should be done for your spirit. When all three of these are managed and boundaries have been in place, then we move closer to wholeness. Personal worship is the key to liberation and the avenue for spiritual health. Richard Foster in *Celebration of Disciplines* says:

> Worship is the human response to the divine initiative. In Genesis God walked in the garden, seeking out Adam and Eve. In the crucifixion Jesus drew men and women to himself (John 12: 32). Scripture is replete with examples of God's efforts to initiate, restore, and maintain fellowship with his children. God is like the father of the prodigal who upon seeing his son a long way off, rushed to welcome him home. Worship is our response to the overtures of love from the heart of the Father. Its central reality is found "in spirit and truth." It is kindled within us only when the Spirit of God touches our human spirit."[33]

---

[33] (Foster, 1998)

This very intimate and inspiring time with God will release us from the dependency on humanity for things that only divinity can provide. We must not allow any thing to distract us or deter us from quality time in worship. As you are reading this work, many of you have learned how to make physical boundaries a reality. You are exercising and getting proper rest. You are guarding yourself against emotional unrest. You must create a spiritual boundary strong enough to keep people away from time and things that you have strictly for God.

Public worship is also important. I surely wouldn't want to devalue the personal worship that is so important to wholeness and spirituality. It is very important for us to remember that we begin this chapter discovering how to decide where to stay in the ministry you are in or move on to somewhere else. This is important because this will affect your maturation into wholeness and it may influence your spiritual progression. Foster again adds this about public worship:

> …have a willingness to be gathered in the power of the Lord. That is, as an individual I must learn to let go of my agenda, of my concern, of my being blessed, of my hearing the word of God. The language of the gathered fellowship is not "I," but "we." There is a submission to the ways of God. There is a submission to one another in the Christian fellowship. There is a desire for God's life to rise up in the group, not just within the individual. If you are praying for a manifestation of the spiritual gifts, it does not have to come upon you but can come upon anybody and upon the group as a whole if that pleases God. Become of one mind, of one accord.[34]

The power of public worship can be so rewarding. The fresh, new experience in a unified setting means that we have the opportunity to escape the cares and calamities of

---

[34] (Foster, 1998)

the world momentarily at least in our minds, hearts, and spirits. This is why boundaries must be present to reserve rights for this area in your life. Nothing should get in the way of worship. It matters!

Work Matters

Part of our spiritual growth and maturation is the work and service that we give back to God because of who He is and what He has done for us. Many of you may be asking, "How is work considered a spiritual concept?" I would like to suggest that work and worship are closely related and that both of them are bi-products of spiritual growth. The more you grow spiritually, the more you have a desire to work for God and serve Him because you love Him and you are connected to Him in worship. They are both needed in our lives. Worship and work should work in concert with one another. One narrative in the bible that gives a great depiction of this relationship involving worship and work is found in the gospel of Luke in chapter 10:38-42:

> 38As Jesus and the disciples continued on their way to Jerusalem, they came to a certain village where a woman named Martha welcomed him into her home. 39 Her sister, Mary, sat at the Lord's feet, listening to what he taught. 40 But Martha was distracted by the big dinner she was preparing. She came to Jesus and said, "Lord, doesn't it seem unfair to you that my sister just sits here while I do all the work? Tell her to come and help me."41 But the Lord said to her, "My dear Martha, you are worried and upset over all these details! 42There is only one thing worth being concerned about. Mary has discovered it, and it will not be taken away from her."[35]

We see clearly Mary had chosen worship and Martha her sister had chosen to work. Now in this passage Jesus simply tells her that she has missed her timing to be

---

[35] (Bible.com, 2008)

concerned with work but he does not rebuke her because she was working. He shows her preference over punishment. Worship should be priority over work, but they are connected. This was not the first time that Jesus was in their house, and this is not the first time that a meal was prepared. Martha was obviously the one being hospitable. I submit the idea that they both are needed. If Mary and Martha were both engaged in worship, none of the work would get done. Conversely, if all were super busy doing church work or any other work all the time, there would be no time to spend with the creator. As our lives become more demanding and we become occupied with trivial tasks, we must reserve the area in our lives that allows us the opportunity to work for the Lord. Sometimes we become so busy serving at our local churches or in our local community groups that we forget why we work in the first place. If we are not careful, we will begin to work for people's approval and not God's approval. To add, some of us work too much. We find no boundaries in our lives regarding working for God simply because we feel that we owe him so much. Our amount of work verses the amount of debt we are in toward God, doesn't even compare. We don't have enough time or energy to really pay God back. Sometimes we have to know our limitations. Quality not quantity is important when it comes to working for God.

Chapter 4:
Relationship Boundaries

"Imagination and perspective create the stage for relationships. We set the stage by how we picture God, the world, and ourselves. The pieces of furniture on the stage are the perspectives we have on life. Relationships are how we then respond to God and react to others on the stage"[36]

-David Eckman

    I would like to say I'm a nice guy. I'd like to think that I pretty much get along with or can befriend anyone. After all I was raised with a sort of kind-hearted pedigree. I enjoy being around people, and from what I've heard from

---

[36] (Eckman, 2005)

others is that I'm pretty good company as well. I enjoy building new relationships and meeting new people. I'm that guy that walks in a room and just like a public announcement, will herald my phone number across the room. I love people and I love it when they love me back. I'm a people's guy. I've been blessed to have the opportunity to pastor a wonderful church, Zion Christian Ministries in the beautiful city of Murfreesboro Tennessee. I'm also bi-vocational; I work in the local school system. I'm an author, teacher, preacher, pastor, and God has blessed my wife Toya and I with three beautiful children. Chris Jr. (C.J.) loves to read, is a straight A student, is involved in ministry, and is a three sport athlete. Jerell, my middle son is unique in his own way. He plays football and constantly reminds me that he is going to be the next pastor at our church. And then there is Taraja. She is the personality of the three. She loves to be the boss and keep her brothers in check. She is in gymnastics and loves to dance. Toya and I are blessed. I could literally write a book on how much I love my wife but suffice it to say, she is my best friend and the love of my life. The point I'm making here is that these are the most important relationships in my life. These are the people that hold me together. It's a full time emotional, spiritual, and also physical job just balancing each of these relationships. It takes work, dedication, patience, and effort. Now these are just four relationships to manage. The load gets heavier when we try to embrace or entertain more. More often than not, many of us are trying to balance those relationships and much more.

I remember coming home one Friday after work and sitting calmly on my couch in front of the TV with a sense of accomplishment after a long hard day. At last a moment to rest. Within minutes, I got a text message from a church member needing my presence at the hospital. I had already agreed to watch a game that night with some of the other church leaders. Taraja climbed up in my lap, and totally unconcerned with the emails and texts I had received she asked, "Daddy, can we have family night tonight?" Thinking swiftly about everything that was pending that night I said to her, "We'll see baby girl, we'll see." I moved slowly to my bedroom and saw my suit lying on the bed, which reminded me that I had a funeral to attend the next day. Right before I got ready to lay down for a quick nap, C.J. made it his business to rush and tell me, "Daddy, don't forget I have a game tonight!" I heard the door open and the cheer "Mommy's home" as Toya walked through the door. She came in the room and asked, "Hey, did you get that email from Jerell's teacher?" I told her I hadn't. "Well, she wants to have a phone conference with us tonight!" I was about to throw in the towel, but I told her that it would be great to give the teacher a call. Toya stared at me and must have sensed that I was on edge. "Are you ok?" She asked. "You look tired. Let's get a sitter tomorrow and just hangout it will be fun!" I replied "great." Now this would have to be after the funeral the next day and it is the weekend, and the thought of me preaching three times on Sunday hit me like a ton of bricks. Let's add to this that there were a couple of members not too pleased with me because they felt like I should just be available to them whenever. I went to the bathroom, closed the door and just cried. This was too much. I couldn't possibly absorb all of this. My mind was in overdrive. I needed help in the worst way. And there, in the bathroom, on that Friday evening I knew that if I had made boundaries in every other area of my life that what was obviously necessary was for me to erect boundaries with all of these relationships.

Relationship boundaries are a must. We must carefully observe every relationship and decide who will have our ear, how far they can go, and what we are or are not willing to give up in order to be in relationship with that individual.

People will drain you quicker than anything else. If you let them, people will leave you depressed, stressed, and angry. I want to help you place the people that you are in relationship with in their respected places. If you don't use boundaries with people in your life, they will create their own. That is a disaster waiting to happen. A couple of years ago, I did a teaching on balancing relationships. In that teaching, I gave a guide to recognizing the motives of the relationships you may have. The people in your life that you are in relationship with are in it to win it, in it to get it, in it to rent it, or in it for you!

In It to Win It!

One of my favorite movies, *Remember the Titans,* tells a story about how a high school football team changed the climate and culture of Alexandria, Virginia which was a place divided by racial tension. A young white man, Gerry Bertier was the senior linebacker, team captain, and obvious leader of all the whites on the team. The antagonist Julius Campbell was the other senior linebacker on the team and it was quite clear that he was the leader of all of the African American players on the team. This team was rather reflective of the tensions that were apparent in the community. Those tensions would often surface in practice until eventually it created this staggering loser type stigma on the team. The whites wouldn't block for the blacks, and the blacks wouldn't block for the whites. They just couldn't seem to come together. They couldn't win! The team had been practicing for a while and the same racial tensions were present. In an attempt to promote unity amongst the players the coach issued an assignment for each player to learn some details about other players on the team that they may not know anything about. By no accident, Gerry and Julius were paired with each other. After a long hard practice that day the two met up just to get this over with. Gerry started in on Julius by telling him how he is a "waste of talent" because he doesn't listen to anyone and how that leaves his teammates out to dry. Julius's response was interesting. He asked him a series of questions, "You're the captain right? You have a job to do? Then why don't you tell your white buddies to block? And I'm supposed to sacrifice myself for the team? What team?" They both had valid points. With a stunned and confused look on his face Gerry's reply was, "See man, that's the worst attitude I've ever heard." Agreeing in an a half sarcastic nod, Julius replied, "Attitude reflects leadership, captain!" Gerry gave him back a puzzled stare. It was evident that he had gotten the message though. Later that night the team was well into their third practice of the day. As usual, none of the black players would work hard for the white players and none of the white players would block for the black players. Then on one toss play, one of the white players, Ray, who had lined up to play tight end missed a block and the running back, who happened to be black, was tackled for a loss in the backfield. Suddenly, Gerry came over and shouted, "What was that Ray? Whatever it is, it ain't blocking!" Gerry said other things I'd rather not repeat but he let Ray know that he better not miss the block again. This was the first time the white team captain had corrected a white teammate for not blocking for a black player. "Line up, do it again!" the coach exclaimed. The quarterback took the snap, tossed the ball and Pete, the running back took the toss and out of nowhere Julius came and leveled him. Pete didn't like that. This was the first time that the apparent black leader had showed any aggression toward another black player.

The two leaders came together with a team chant that would eventually be in seed form the turning of a whole city. The other players were dead silent as they watched. What exactly was happening? Two enemies united on common ground. The team witnessed two warring sides find a compromise. So the question is worth asking, what is strong enough to unite even enemies? What kind of thing can hold a relationship between two people that seem to be like oil and water? The answer is simple yet powerful. A cause. A cause can bring people together who otherwise wouldn't even speak to each other. Two people who are complete opposites will sit all of that aside in order to accomplish a task or to bring fulfillment to a cause. In this case, their cause was winning. In order to win, the team had to come together.

There will be people in your life that have come just to win. Some common interest that you have, or a dream that is synonymous with their dream will cause them to want to spend time with you and be in your life. These relationships are built around what both of you are in pursuit of. Many marriages are built on people who are just in it to win it. The spouse is only there because both of you want finer things in life and it's just logical that both of your incomes together would be one step closer to that cause. For a pastor, you have people who share similar ideas about ministry; they love where you are headed so they stick around because you're on the same path that they are on. What about certain co-workers on your job? Face it; the only reason why you talk to them is because you sit next to them in the cubicle everyday at work. Be careful with the "in it to win it bunch." Don't expect more from them than what they will give. They are in it for something other than the relationship. There is something else that is the basis of the relationship. If you remove the cause, or if your heart changes on a matter, you get a new job, change your thoughts on some things, or if you have a personal growth moment, then these people will leave you. They are only with you because you share a common pursuit. Once that is gone so are they, so you need clear boundaries for these people in your life. Never give them in-depth access to your heart and conversation. Draw a very precise boundary for them. Keep them connected to the cause and that's it. Don't let them too close because they may see your frailty and humanity, and it may threaten their idea of the success that comes with the cause. There are some conversations that just simply aren't appropriate with this group. There is no need to share with them your inner thoughts. They shouldn't be privy to your personal preferences. It is hardly necessary for them to know your emotions or moods. When you talk to them, keep the conversation limited to what is necessary to carry out your tasks. After all, that's all that is required. As long as you are winning, they will be beneficial for you. If you keep safe boundaries with this group, even when you are not winning, it will not matter because you haven't given them that much power and prestige in your life. Boundary drawn!

In it To Get It!

After ten years of ministry and nearly twenty years of watching my father in ministry, I've gained much insight as to why people relationally connect with others. I have certainly examined and experienced instances where people really reveal their relationship status. As we have already mentioned, there is a purpose or a cause that unites certain people. To move a step further, some people are in it to get it. Who knows what the "it" is. We all have been gifted with certain qualities or have certain attributes that are necessary for us to operate in purpose and in excellence for a particular cause or mandate. That could describe your "it." Many will try and immolate you or duplicate your lifestyle and giftedness. To be honest, there are some people that may benefit more from your company than you do from theirs. Typically, these people will make it known that you add value to their life and they will show you with their actions. They very rarely add substance to your situation. In my career field, I have people share this with me all the time whether purposely or indirectly. They will say things like "you helped me with that" or "I've learned so much from you!" These are typically people that are in the direct career field or aspiring to do what you do one day. If you are the boss in your organization then it is the team under you. If you are a pastor, it is your ministry team. If you are a worship leader, it's the others that serve along side you. If you're a school teacher, it is the other teachers on the staff. We all have these people. They want to get it! They will do what is necessary to get it. They will make enough time to hang around you, they will use you, take advantage of you, and they will often never consider your best interest. They will just stay dedicated to what they can get from you. That's the reason why you have to draw concise boundaries for these individuals. If they are there to take and withdraw from you, then you have to make a decision on what you are willing to give and how much you are ready to give up. You will always have takers, but the question is do you also have a boundary for them?

Be careful with this bunch. You will have to organize interactions with them. Make sure you plan out your meetings and exposure to them. If your information is quality, put your own value on it. Charge them for it. Never hide behind these fake relationships, giving to them freely what others would pay for. Don't try to live up to their expectations for you. Create your own expectations that you have for them. After all, they are coming to you not the other way around. Limit their exposure to your giftedness.

In It to Rent It!

I remember a brief season of my ministry that was really difficult for me to understand. In our third year, Zion Christian Ministries was unusually beginning to lose people. My mind was all over the place trying to figure out what was happening. How could this be? Why were people making the decision to move on to something or someone else? Another question that was pressing me was, how did I not see this coming? I remember one night I had become very emotional because a woman that had helped start the ministry decided to leave. We were on good terms, she was not upset, and there wasn't any scandal to report. I thought she was happy with everything that was happening. At the end of the day, she simply felt that her time there was up. I took it personal, and I felt betrayed. I know that I shouldn't have. She met with me and explained that she was fine, and that she had nothing against the ministry. She felt that one day our ministry would be thriving and that it is already blessed. She just knew that it was time for her to move on. Shortly after that, while preparing for a leadership conference, I was still emotionally attached to the loss of this person. I had been in prayer that God would release me from this person and just let her go but it wasn't that easy. I felt attached. I felt that I had in some sense lost a child. Then while in my study I came across these passages of scripture:

Care for the flock that God has entrusted to you. Watch over it willingly, not grudgingly—not for what you will get out of it, but because you are eager to serve God. (1 Peter 5:2)

Don't lord it over the people assigned to your care, but lead them by your own good example. (1 Peter 5:3)

These words literally leaped out of the pages at me. Notice the directives in these passages. "Care for the Flock that God has entrusted you." Then it goes on to say "watch over it." The other statement in verse 3 "the people assigned to your care" is what really did it for me. Wait! I get it now! They aren't my people. They are God's people not mine. People are just assigned to me. This means that when God is ready, he could re-assign them. More succinctly, there are people who will not take ownership of the vision; they will just rent the vision. From experience I can tell you that some people will be here today and gone tomorrow. Some people come in your life with the intention of leaving. They are renting. They know that it will be a temporary relationship.

Draw your boundary with the renters. You have to be careful not to make long-term investments in people who will only be there for a short time. Don't give permanent information to temporary people. Don't give ownership privileges to individuals that are leasing. It will be a waste of your time and energy to try and invest in people who will leave you at any minute. Renters use you for what they need and they always keep in mind that you and your cause are only necessary items that will help them get what they desire. Treat, handle, and communicate with them that way. Only tell them information that is shared with the general public. Don't include them in your future plans. Don't allow them to control the decisions you make for your future, and never let them influence how you should feel about yourself. Feed them information as if they will not be around long. This boundary will help you maintain control of your life and keep you sane and whole.

In it For You

Although we have covered the fact that you will have relationships with people who are in it for all the wrong reasons, there are those that are authentic in their relationships. There are some people that are genuinely in the relationship for you. They are in it to win it but even if you are not winning, they are still there. They are in it to get it, but even if you don't have it, they are still there. They are in it to rent it at first, and then they grow into ownership. Your hurts become their hurts. Your pains become their pains. They are totally committed to you. They love you! Yet, even still, you have to draw boundaries for this group as well. Sometimes the very ones that are in it for us and the ones that love us the most are the ones that burden us the most. You must put a boundary on them as well so that they will not become the filler of a void that only God can fill in your life. The reason why we have to put a boundary on them is because they actually do have our ears, they are dear to our hearts, and they are owners not renters. This means that we will hold a deeper level of respect for what they will say to us. Not all of the advice will be good for us! Sometimes we will take unsound advice from people who are not learned but they are loyal. This is dangerous. We will take relationship advice from people who have poor relationships only because we know that when all else fails they are committed to the relationship. As you are reading this you are also thinking of some people that you may have allowed to have too much say in your life simply because they are family, or you have been long time friends, or maybe you have both been through so much together that it's hard for you not to trust what they say. I would encourage you to have a boundary for them as well. They may be experts in something or maybe they are better than you in certain areas of life. It is still going to prove to be wise for you to pick and choose how far they can go in dictating your actions, attitudes, or aptitudes. Remember that although they may be faithful to you, they are far from perfect. Your life is already filled with pains, problems, or pressures so you can't afford to have them project their fears or failures on you. This is a very tough boundary to implement. Relationship that have withstood the test of time and trials often develop a deeper level of trust between those involved. However, trust is not equivalent to truth. It is possible for those we trust to just be wrong about certain things and it is possible for them to give us damaging advice. Many times, we receive their words, (not because they were right) because we were feeling a sense of duty because of the duration of the relationship. Just remember, even though they are "in it for me" I'm not obligated to move when they say, act how they say, or listen to every piece of advice. That's not companionship, that's control.

Finally, it should be clear that all of us need boundaries in order to experience any level of wholeness.

This kind of life does not just happen, it has to be intentional. Dear reader, your sanity and peace are at stake. This book has been your invitation to live life with boundaries!

References

Bible.com. 2008. *Holy Bible (NLT).* Prod. Life.Church. Oklahoma City, OK, October 20.

Carol S. Dweck, Ph.D. 2006. *Mindset.* New York, NY: Ballantine Books.

Dictionary.com, LLC. 2016. *Dictionary.com.* January 1. Accessed February 17, 2016. www.dictionary.com.

Eckman, David. 2005. *Becoming Who God Intended.* La Habra, CA: The Lockman Foundation.

Evans, Tony. 2012. *Kingdom Man.* Carol Stream, IL: Tyndale House Publishers.

Foster, Richard J. 1998. *Celebration of Disciplines.* 20th Anniversary Edition. Toronto, ON: HarperCollins Publishers.

Heath, Chip Heath and Dan. 2012. *Switch.* New York, NY: Broadway Books.

Hutchcraft, Ron. 2004. *Called to Greatness.* Celebration Edition. Chicago, IL: Moody Publishers.

III, Ben Witherington. 2010. *Jesus and Money.* Grand Rapids, MI: Brazos Press.

Jenkins, Lee. 2001. *Taking Care of Business.* Chicago, IL:
    Moody Press.

Maxwell, John C. 2007. *Talent is Never Enough.* Nashville,
    Tennessee: Thomas Nelson.

Richard A. Swenson, M.D. 2004. *Margin.* Revised Edition.
    Colorado Springs, CO: Nav Press.

Rubin, Jordan S. 2009. *The Maker's Diet for Weight Loss.*
    Lake Mary, Florida: Siloam.

Ryan, M.J. 2012. *AZ Quotes.* January 10. Accessed 2016.
    www.azquotes.com.

Spirituality, Emotionally Healthy. 2006. *Peter Scazzero.*
    Grand Rapids, Michigan: Zondervan.

Swindoll, Charles R. 1987. *Living Above the Level of
    Mediocrity.* Nashville, TN: Thomas Nelson.

Made in the USA
Columbia, SC
28 August 2024